THE
SONG

CHARLOTTE ZOLOTOW
ILLUSTRATED BY NANCY TAFURI

GREENWILLOW BOOKS · NEW YORK

**Library of Congress
Cataloging in Publication Data**
Zolotow, Charlotte (date)
The song.
    Summary: Throughout the year,
Susan hears a little bird inside
her singing of the changing
seasons, but no one else can hear it.
[1. Seasons—Fiction]
I. Tafuri, Nancy, ill.
II. Title.
PZ7.Z77Sr   [E]   81-6357
ISBN 0-688-00618-3   AACR2
ISBN 0-688-00817-8 (lib. bdg.)

THE
SONG

One day Susan woke up
with the song of a little bird
inside her.

He sang sunshine and
leaves rustling in the branches,
and he sang roses with sweet smells,
and butterflies and clover
and lilacs dripping with rain.
He sang mountains far away
and meadows filled
with daisies and buttercups.
"Listen," Susan said to her mother.
"Listen," she said to her father.
But neither of them heard.

All summer the little bird sang.

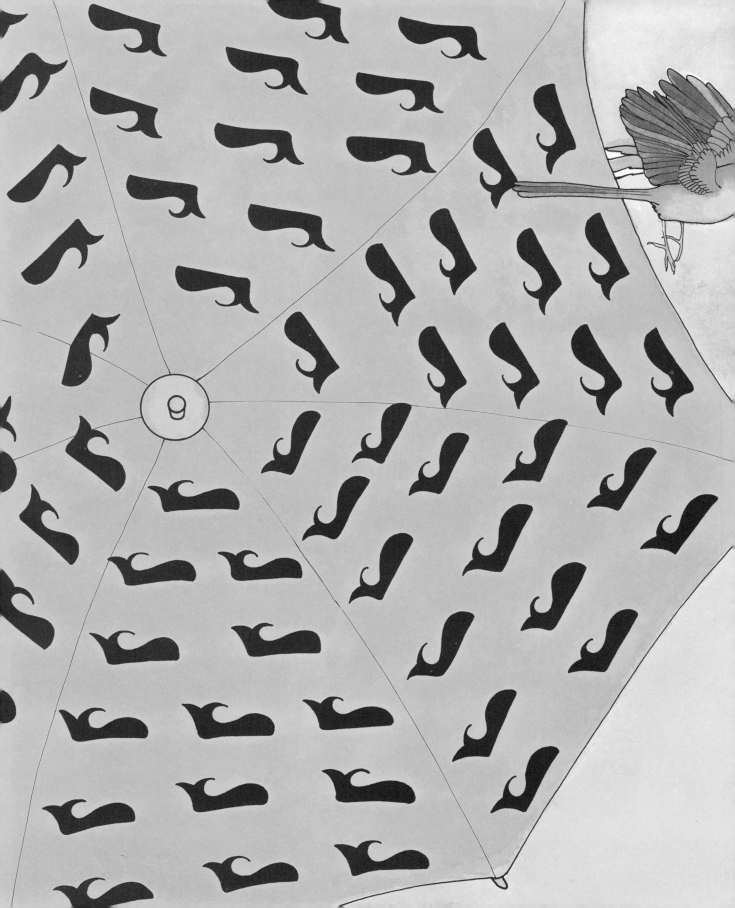

And one day his song began
to change to maple leaves
and tangles of red and orange
in the garden
and goldenrod
and the beginning of school.
"Listen," Susan said to her mother.
"Listen," Susan said to her father.
But neither of them
could hear the bird singing.
The bird sang about the leaves
falling from the trees and
pumpkins and bittersweet
and rusty chrysanthemums.

He sang cold winds
and gray skies
and the feeling
of something about to end
and something that would begin.

"Listen, listen!" Susan said.
But her mother and father
couldn't hear what she heard.
"Susan," they said,
"there is no bird,
there is no bird."

Fall was over
and the little bird began to sing in white.
He sang of snowflakes and frosty windows
and the sting of the wind.
He sang of wood fires burning
and the splutter of the flames
and toasted marshmallows.
He sang of pine trees
and mistletoe and holly.
"Oh, listen, listen," the little girl said.
But no one else could hear.

The little bird sang all winter,

and then he began to sing
of jonquils and hyacinths.
He sang of silky new grass
and the smell of wet earth.
He sang of violets and other birds
and buds along the branches.
He sang of golden and yellow forsythia.

It was a warm soft spring song,
and Susan listened to him
as she walked home from school.
On the way she met a friend.
"Listen," she said,
"do you hear what I hear?"
"I hear a bird singing," he said,
"and he's singing new grass
and the smell of wet earth
and the softness in the air."
"Yes," said Susan,
"and he's singing pink clouds
and apple blossoms and
the stirrings of things."

The notes in the little bird's song went higher,
and he sang about putting a stick in front of
a fuzzy caterpillar who climbed up one side
of it and down the other as though it were
a little bridge.

He sang about playing ball and jumping rope
and Susan's dog who ran out to meet them
as they walked home together.

F.E.
LER ISS A
LUZ